BEST WISHE 9-

Peter Paul Lucote

AVOCADO MAGIC

Peter Paul Licata

authorHOUSE®

AuthorHouse™
1663 Liberty Drive
Bloomington, IN 47403
www.authorhouse.com
Phone: 1-800-839-8640

First published by AuthorHouse 4/16/2010

ISBN: 978-1-4520-0823-3 (e)
ISBN: 978-1-4520-0822-6 (sc)

Library of Congress Control Number: 2010904374

Printed in the United States of America
Bloomington, Indiana

This book is printed on acid-free paper.

God kissed Fallbrook, California.

That's what the residents will tell you. So it only makes sense that angels like to frequent the area. The heavenly visitors come to Fallbrook with a great affinity for its friendly, kind, angelic like inhabitants. The folks in this rural community lovingly tend to the lush groves and peaceful orchids among the gently rolling hills of their emerald paradise. And the land returns the love.

The angels come to watch, observe, learn and on occasion help these most deserving people.

Lance Rutter and his two children Maura-Jean and Billy live on an avocado farm in Fallbrook

1

located in Northern San Diego County off Highway 15 just west of Duke Snyder Road.

It is evening with a clear sky in late September. Lance is standing in a lighted area on a mound of dirt exactly sixty feet and six inches from a scarecrow with a baseball bat who is standing on the right side of a handmade wooden home plate in front of a few bales of hay. He is staring down the scarecrow the family calls Russell and shaking off signs. His two children are watching.

"Why are you throwing avocado pits instead of baseballs, Dad?" Maura, Lances's twelve year old daughter asked.

"The only baseball I found was half eaten by mice. The only thing I could throw is a sinker. They must have eaten the top half of the baseball."

"Star bright make a wish tonight," Billy, Lances six year old boy said. The darkened sky was full of activity as the Delta Aurigids meteor shower was performing this evening.

"Why don't you just buy some new baseballs?" Maura asked.

"Not so fast there," Lance said. "Baseballs cost money and we got to be careful with our money. The good Lord has blessed us over time with this bountiful land, but for the last couple of years we haven't made any money. The land is going through a cleansing I think. The drought and fires hurt us bad."

"Wouldn't too much rain be more like a cleansing?" Maura asked.

"Ugh...This is more like a dry cleaning," Lance said. "Although I got to admit I made some mistakes...with the banks, the fertilizer, tryin' to manage this farm. Your mother did all that, it was easy for her. I don't have your mother's brain. May she rest in peace. That woman was a saint. And smart."

"You're doing all right, Daddy," Maura said. "I know it's not easy."

Lance wound up, displaying the form he had when he started as a promising pitcher for the Albuquerque Isotopes, a minor league baseball team affiliated with the Los Angeles Dodgers. He was on injured reserve now. He nodded his head approving the pitch selection from the imaginary catcher and delivered a breaking avocado pit that caught the corner of the plate.

"Strike one," Billy proclaimed acting like a four foot umpire.

"Dad, that was pretty good," Maura said. "What's goin' on, why are you out here tonight?"

"Well," Lance took a deep breath, "Joe Torre called the other day. Joe's' currently the Dodgers manager, he was the pitching coach when I first signed with the Isotopes."

"I thought Joe Torre was the New York Yankees manager, Dad," Maura said. "Didn't he win a lot of World Series for them."

"Yes he did. Fine man. Great manager."

Lance cupped the pit with both hands, turning it like a real baseball as his fingers gripped the imaginary threads and threw another one.

"Strike two," Billy said.

"Then why did the Yankees fire Joe Torre?" Maura asked.

Lance scratched his head. "I guess because he won so much George Steinbrenner wanted to give someone else a chance."

His daughter didn't seem satisfied with the answer. "That doesn't make much sense," she said.

With a grin, Lance continued his story. "Anyway, Joe Torre tells me the other day the Dodgers may need a right handed pitcher with a good breaking ball. They have a lot of injuries and they started to look for someone."

"That's fantastic, Dad," Maura said.

Lance shook off several signs that weren't there to start with and delivered an avocado

Peter Paul Licata

pit that looked liked it would hit Russell but caught the corner of the plate.

"Very nice pitch, Dad!" Maura said.

"You otta dar, battah!" Billy screeched.

"It's still a long shot," Lance said. "But if it comes I gotta be ready. Nothing to do in the field except bury dead avocado trees. That's depressing. Oh the money would be God sent if I get the call. I gotta tell you kids our finances are not in good shape. No, no, I'm sorry to say we're not in good shape."

"I could quit school and get a job," Billy said. "What do I need second grade for?"

"You just wanna quit school," Maura said.

"Well," the boy replied with a shrug, "now I got a good reason to quit."

"You're not quitting school, Billy, forget that thought," Maura said. "But it's ok to marry a rich girl from your first grade class if you find one. In the meantime we will find a way. We'll be all right. Won't we, Dad."

"Sure we will, honey. We'll be fine. It would be nice to have a little magic to help us through these tough times. I certainly wouldn't refuse some magic."

The kids had heard their father talk about financial problems before. They had heard him ask for a bit of magic over and over again. Maura was actually starting to help her father manage the farm. She was proficient with numbers, excellent with the employees, and skilled with all aspects of the operation – pretty good for a twelve year old. She was very smart and her Dad...well, he wasn't, but he worked his tail off and was a loving and devoted father. Maura, it seemed, had inherited her mother's vast intelligence.

"Star bright make a wish tonight," Billy said.

"Nice pitch, Dad," Maura said. "That one broke strong and dove for the plate."

"Yeah, I'm startin' to loosen up. I'm startin' to feel better."

"Is your shoulder all right, Dad?" Maura asked.

Lance winked at her. "Yeah, it feels good."

Billy followed a frog down the path toward a small clearing where he played and had a tent set up. "Star bright make a wish tonight," he said as he watched another meteor fall through the sky. He closed his eyes and made a wish. Then he opened them. Nothing. "What the hell does a guy have to do to get a little magic around here?" Billy asked.

"Just ask," the voice behind Billy said. "What do you want the magic for, Billy?"

Startled, the boy jumped backwards. "Who are you?" he asked. "I hope you are a magician!"

"Sorry. I'm not a magician. I'm an angel."

"You are an angel," Billy said, his jaw hanging open. "You look like a kid the same age as me."

It was Billy's first angel encounter and they could be tricky at any age.

"I am, I'm six just like you."

"Can you do magic?"

"Yes, I can do magic."

Billy looked skeptical. "Prove it."

Suddenly the young angel wasn't Billy's size anymore but a figure over fifteen feet tall! He now loomed large over the boy.

"Wow, I can't do magic like that, the best I could do is pull a quarter out of my ear." Billy strained his neck to see all of the vision before him. "You probably know the quarter trick, huh?"

"Yeah, I do. My name is Brent." The angel returned to former size.

"How did you know my name?" Billy asked, the question just now coming to him. "You're a smart angel aren't you?"

Brent smiled. "Yes, I am a smart angel."

"Can I be an angel some day? My sister says I'm almost as smart as my dad."

"Smart helps, but it takes more than being smart, Billy."

"What does it take?"

"It takes heart. A good heart. A kind heart. A generous heart. A noble heart. Your father has heart, Billy."

Billy cocked his head. "Is he gonna be an angel?"

"Oh, I don't know. It's possible."

"I didn't know angels could be so young, plus most of the angels I see in books have wings."

"My mom and dad were a big help with me being an angel," Brent explained, "and the only time we wear our wings is for formal pictures. Why are you asking for magic, Billy?"

"My dad may have a good heart and a good arm but he's got a sick wallet. I know he works real hard but we might have to sell the farm and move to Alaska and become ice farmers. My dad is tryin to join the Dodgers so he can strike out the Big Opple and beat the Yankees and make money."

"I see," the angel said, nodding his head. "How's your sister doing?"

"She needs help. I think she needs a new brain. She wants me to get married." Billy made a face that looked like he might get sick.

"Oh, I think your sister is kidding with you."

Now Billy seemed very serious. "Can you help us, Brent?" he asked.

"Yes, I'm sure we can. Let me talk to my mom and dad."

Billy ran to his GI Joe tent and returned with a large plastic jug. "Should I use this?" he asked.

"What's that, Billy?"

"It's my magic potion," the boy replied. "Only the magic part isn't workin'."

"What's in there?"

"Mentos, olive oil, cherries and coffee."

"Mentos! Is that the stuff they play with on You Tube?" Brent asked.

"Yeah, that's the same stuff."

"Yes, Billy, you can use your magic potion. Hold it up over your head."

Billy raised the jug over his head with two hands. The angel pointed his finger toward the jug and a silver ray of light danced on the concoction.

"What did you do it?" Billy asked, his .eyes wide.

"It's a secret."

"What should I do with it?"

"Let it cook overnight. And then...you'll know what do to with it. I promise."

"OK," Billy said.

"Billy. Billy!" Lance yelled from the top of the path. "Come on, we're going inside."

"Want to come in and have some ice cream and meet my dad and sister?" Billy asked the angel.

"Thank you, I'd love to," Brent said with a smile only an angel could make. "But I really have to get going. We will meet again. I promise."

"Goodbye Brent."

"Goodbye Billy. I wish you and your family much happiness."

The angel vanished quickly. Billy walked up the path and met his father.

"What's going on down there, Billy?" Lance asked. "Are you playin' with the big flashlight down there?"

"No," Billy replied. "I was talking to an angel."

"You were! Was Spiderman or the Green Hornet with him?"

"No. Just the angel. He's gonna help us with some magic."

"That's just great, Billy," his father said with a laugh.

The next morning, Maura was in the kitchen making pancakes for Billy, and toast for her father. Lance had put handrails with shelves in the kitchen and made some alterations to the stove to make it easier for her when she was in the kitchen. Maura loved to cook. Maura loved to live.

"Where's my red shirt?" asked Billy.

"It's dirty," Maura said. "I'm gonna wash clothes after school. Wear the blue one."

Their father called from upstairs, "Maura, did you see my work pants?"

"They're in the dryer, Dad."

"Where's my book bag?" Billy asked from another room.

"In the hallway near the door," Maura replied.

"Maura, I won't be able to pick you up today I have a dentist appointment, "Lance said.

"That's next week, Dad."

"Oh, ok."

Then Maura noticed a leak in the faucet. "Oh shoot...What a time for plumbing problems." She grabbed a wrench and a screwdriver, took the pancakes off the heated stove surface and attacked the disorderly sink.

The phone rang. And rang. And rang.

"Could someone get that please?" Maura asked. No answer.

Maura picked up the phone. "Hello."

"Would you like to take a short survey and be eligible to win tickets to the circus?" the woman asked.

Maura had no time for this right now. "Could you please call back, I'm a little busy now," she said.

"Sure."

Maura hung up the phone just as Dad came into the kitchen.

"How's your morning goin', sunshine?" he asked Maura as he took his seat at the table.

"All right, Dad."

"The weather report is callin' for rain. Yesterday they said no chance for rain for at least a week. Rain, Maura, ain't that great."

"Sure is, what are you gonna do today, Dad?"

"Make sure all the farm equipment is workin' proper."

"Billy, your pancakes are ready," Maura yelled. "Here ya go, Dad, avocado toast, avocado tea and some avocado slices."

"I'm gonna take this in the barn to eat," Lance said, "I want to start checking the equipment."

"See you after school, Dad."

"Sure thing, Maura, love ya."

A letter came for Lance that morning. But it never reached him. Maura, with her father's approval, handled all the mail. She also paid the bills, cleaned the house--usually a room or two a day--and kept everyone on schedule. She was the Rutter family's glue. Maura read the letter sent to her father:

Dear Lance Rutter,

I am compelled by law to send this notice. The California Department of Children's Wellness has been informed of a "possible" infraction of the Children's Wellness Code and therefore must initiate investigative procedures in this matter.

Maura Rutter, our records state, is afflicted with Muscular Dystrophy. Maura, like many children and adults who have MD, has special needs. We have information that has Maura working in the avocado groves on your farm. While I am sure there is a valid explanation this situation raises questions which must be addressed.

Mr. Rutter, I assure you the action taken by myself and this department are for the benefit of your daughter Maura. I hope to visit you and your family as soon as my mobility returns. I was just in an accident and suffered a broken leg.

Thank you for your understanding in this matter.

Joan Miller

Executive Director

California Department of Children's Wellness

Working in the fields, Maura thought. What are they talking about? Maura decided she would answer the letter for her father.

Miss Joan Miller,

Yes, I am sure someone saw my daughter Maura along with my son Billy in the orchards with me. They like to help as much as possible. I was not so keen on the idea at first but Maura persisted and I gave in. Maura insists it is not work for her. She calls her time in the sun-drenched orchards her special time. She likes helping and I limit her duties. Maura knows that her time in the orchards may be limited. She likes being with me and her brother in the peaceful countryside. She say's Muscular Dystrophy is a thief so she must guard her special time.

You are welcome to come to our house, to go with us in the orchards, if you would like. Come. Come with an open heart.

I am sorry to hear of your unfortunate accident and I wish you a speedy recovery.

Sincerely,

Lance Rutter.

"I can't believe how big they are," Lance said holding and admiring an avocado while sitting at the dinner table. "They grew so quick, not even a week. Even the dead trees undied and came back to life. And they're simply delicious. I don't understand it."

"It's magic," Billy said. "I asked the angel for a little magic and he delivered."

"What are you talking about, Billy?" Maura asked while putting a cheeseburger on Billy's plate. "Were you praying when you did this."

"No. Could I have some more soda please."

"Here you go, Dad, just the way you like your burgers," Maura said, putting a gigantic hamburger, which was actually the new crop of avocado mixed together with bread and spices then grilled, on his plate. Maura added a sprinkle of ground beef on top. Lance was eating these since he could remember.

"Billy, will you please tell us what you are talkin' about?" Lance asked. "When did this happen?"

"The night you were throwing avocado pits to Russell I saw an angel down near my tent. I didn't believe him at first. I asked him to prove he was an angel. He was the same size as me and then all of a sudden he was as tall as the oak tree. Do we have any potato chips?"

"Why didn't you say something about this, Billy?" Maura asked.

"I did. I told Dad."

Lance raised an eyebrow. "You did?"

"Yeah. You asked me if Spiderman and the Green Hornet were with the angel."

"Were they?" Lance asked.

"No."

Maura gave Lance an incredulous look. "Billy, are you making up stories again?"

"No."

"Honest to God, Billy?" Maura asked.

"Honest to God," Billy swore.

"What do you think, Dad?" asked Maura.

"This is the tastiest burger I ever had," Lance said, then taking a big drink of his avocado ice tea.

"That's great," Maura said, "but I meant what do you think about Billy's story?"

"Quite a story that's for sure. I do believe you saw something, Billy, but what it was I'm not sure."

"Is there anything else that happened, Billy?" Maura asked.

"I asked the angel if I should use the magic potion I made," Billy said.

"Magic potion, what magic potion?" asked Lance.

"I made a magic potion because I heard you say we could use a little magic. I showed it to the angel and he put a shiny light on it and it started to fizzle and then it got smoky. I said what should I do with this and he said let it cook overnight and then you'll know what to do with it."

Maura looked her brother in the eye, not sure whether or not she should believe him. "What did you do with the magic potion?"

"Well, the next day when I looked it was changed."

"How changed?" Lance asked.

"It was a color I never saw before and it smelled."

His father said, "What did it smell like?"

"It smelled like poop," Billy said softly, "so I poured it on the manure pile that you use for fertilizer."

"Dad, did you spread that manure in the grove?" Maura asked.

"Yes, I did, Maura."

Four days later.

"Congratulations, Dad!" Maura said as she slowly approached the makeshift pitching mound in the back yard carrying a small sack. "Billy just told me you got the call to play in the World Series. He's in the house calling, tweeting and e-mailing everyone he knows. That's one happy little boy."

"Thank you, Maura. Well... I did get the call from Joe Torre, they want me on the team, but whether I play or not remains to be seen."

"You'll be ready if you do play, Dad," said his daughter reassuringly. "Look what I got from the baseball coach at school."

"Real baseballs. Coach Morgan gave them to you?"

"Yes, Dad. He sends his best wishes. He heard you might get the call."

"God bless that man," Lance said. "He's an asset to the community. These balls are in good shape, they look like they were hardly used."

"Coach Morgan said the whole team is rooting for you."

Maura stumbled and almost fell.

"Maura, are you okay?" Lance's voice became panicked. "Maura, please tell me the truth."

"The last couple of days I've been a little wobbly. But don't worry, Dad, I'll be all right."

"Oh no, I'm not going to New York if you're not feeling well."

"Yes, you are. I've had these bouts before, they come and go. Most likely you're never going to get this chance again."

"I know you're like your mother, Maura, beautiful, smart and a little stubborn. I know I'll never change your mind. I'm gonna call your Aunt Rose and ask her to stay with you and Billy while I'm in New York."

"OK, Dad. Can I fix you something to eat?"

"Thank you, Maura, but I just had a large avocado salad and a little avocado ice cream that I made last night."

"You're gonna turn into an avocado some day, you eat so much of them," said Maura, laughing.

"I just love them, Maura, and I can't get enough. You and Billy should try the ice cream."

"Maybe later. Billy and I just don't have the massive appetite you have for avocados."

"I know, Maura, but these are different. They're so delicious and they make you feel so good."

Maura smiled at him. "You've been saying that for years, Dad."

Lance smiled back. "OK, go rest."

"Show me what you can do with a real baseball first."

Lance picked up a baseball, went into his windup and threw toward Russell.

"Wow! I've never seen a ball break so much and go over the plate."

"Neither did I, Maura."

Several days later the World Series would start in New York between the Yankees and the Los Angeles Dodgers. The first two games were scheduled in New York, the next three in Los Angeles and if needed the last two in New York. Lance wanted to take his kids to New York but money was tight, school was in session and Maura wasn't feeling well. Billy understood, and he said he would prefer to stay home and help take care of his older sister. The boy thought that was even more important than going to New York, which brought tears to Lance's eyes. This six year old had typical Fallbrook compassion. Lance and Maura would watch the first two games on television. They would attend the games in Los Angeles. The odds makers gave little chance of the Series returning to New York as the powerful Yankees were expected to take the series in no more than five games or maybe sweep in four. The scrappy Dodgers under Joe Torre would have none of that. Torre managed brilliantly and the series was tied at three games each. The last game would be held in New York at Yankee Stadium on a Saturday. Maura who attended the games in LA with Billy, and said she was feeling a little better. She wasn't, but she told everyone she was.

In a mutual display of class when the Dodgers and the Yankees organizations heard what the Rutter family was going through they flew Maura and Billy to New York, paid for their accommodations and provided full-time nursing for Maura all expenses paid, even though she insisted she didn't need it.

Maura surprised her father with her sudden appetite for the newly grown avocados. They tasted good and made her feel better, just like her father had been saying for years. She wasn't so restricted with her physical activity, she felt her muscles starting to work the way they should. These weren't her grandfather's avocados, these were special. These were heaven sent. She packed an ample supply for the trip. Maura even thought to send a box of avocados to Joan Miller of the California Department of Children's Wellness, the woman who had sent the inquiry notice to Lance. It would be a good will package. The accompanying letter said the avocados were from Lance Rutter. He would like to meet with her in the near future and he hoped her broken leg was healing well.

The final game, game seven was before a massive standing room only audience. A battle of Joes. Skippers Joe Torre with the Dodgers and Joe Girardi with the Yankees. The Yankees were hungry for another World Series victory, the Dodgers just as eager to deny them. Joe Torre would love his team to be the spoilers.

Lance had not pitched in any of the first six games but he would be needed for this game as Joe Torre had nearly exhausted his pitching staff. He got the nod as the game's starter. Who... Who is Lance Rutter? That was the question being asked by thousands in the stadium as Lance's name was announced. Torre knew Lance, while getting along with everyone, could be difficult to read his true feelings and therefore manage. Lance was a humble, proud, and somewhat tricky man to truly understand. Torre would take no chances. He saw the bond that existed between father and daughter. He saw how Maura could calm him down when he got riled. He noticed how Maura was dialed into his mechanics and was able to talk him through anything. So Torre was able to hire Maura as an assistant coach since someone on his staff had been hospitalized with bronchitis. He put Maura in a Dodgers uniform and she sat in the dugout with the team next to Torre. Billy was directly behind the dugout where Torre had managed, after some difficulty, to get him a single seat. Torre had a staff member constantly yet discreetly watch him. Billy told Torre he was a big boy and didn't need a babysitter. There were three empty seats, two to the left and one to the right of Billy. Torre was told these four seats were actually reserved by the Heven family who had a little boy of their own and they would gladly allow Billy to sit with them.

"Hi Billy," the little boy said as he took a seat next to him. "Do you remember me?"

Billy's eyes lit up. "Yeah, I remember you. You're Brent, the angel who was in my back yard."

"I told you we would meet again, Billy. I'd like you to meet my parents," Brent said.

"Hi Billy, I'm Trent, Brent's dad and this is Regina his mom."

"Hello Billy," Regina said.

"Are you angels too?" Billy asked.

"Yes we are," Regina whispered, 'but we don't want to make a big deal about it."

"We don't want to be a distraction," Trent explained.

"Are you gonna help my dad and sister beat the Yankees with magic stuff?" Billy asked.

"No we're not, Billy, we don't have to," Regina said.

"Billy, your father and sister are more than capable of winning this game on their own," Trent said. "They don't need our help."

"Brent told us some very nice things about your dad and sister," Regina said. "You should be very proud of them."

"Billy, with the right attitude and hard work you can be anything you want," Trent said. "Never let anybody tell you different."

"I want to be a magician," Billy said.

"I'm sure you will be one of the best magicians ever," Regina said.

"I'm going to give you some magic tips," young Brent said.

"Welcome to game seven of the World Series," Joe Buck said. He was one of the national broadcasters for the game. "It has come down to this. It's up to a thirty-nine year old avocado farmer from Fallbrook, California to bring home the bacon. Joe Torre has put the avocado in his hand, metaphorically speaking. Can he get it done it, Tim?"

"Actually you were right on with your metaphor, Joe," Tim McCarver, Joe Buck's partner in the broadcast booth said. "Word has it that Lance Rutter was practicing with avocado pits because he couldn't afford baseballs. Some say Lance Rutter is about as smart as an avocado. But let me be clear, when he played with the Albuquerque Isotopes he categorically had the best curve ball in the minor leagues, hands down, maybe the best curve ball in all baseball. It was 'that' good. And with a decent fastball there were a lot of predictions this easygoing farmer could be one of the best."

"Then what happened, Tim?" Joe Buck asked.

"Some of the usual culprits," Tim said, "injuries, family needs, and I'm sorry to say his wife died leaving him with two small children and a farm to maintain."

"I don't think the Dodgers' situation is helped in any way by the two year trial period in which this year all pitchers for the National

League and the American League will bat in all games in the World Series," Joe Buck said. "Next year they can go with the designated hitter in all games. It used to be pitchers bat when playing in the National League stadium and a designated hitter utilized in an American League stadium.

"You're right, Joe," Tim said. "This does not help the Dodgers. Hitting was never Lance Rutter's strong suit. So it will be one for the ages if Lance could pull this off."

"It certainly will be, Tim."

"What does he have to do?" Joe Buck asked.

"He has to remain calm, not get riled, and stay with his game plan which is to throw strikes on both sides of the plate and not walk batters; if he does this he has got a chance."

Lance walked the first three batters. "What was Torre thinking?" could be heard over and over again in the crowded stadium. Why couldn't the Dodgers manager find anyone else to pitch other than this unknown farmer. The bases were loaded in the top of the first inning. The Yankees could grab a lead early in the game and with their strong pitching staff that could mean the end of the Dodgers' World Series hopes.

"Torre's got to be questioning his decision to go with Rutter," Joe Buck said.

"Yes I think you're right, Joe," Tim McCarver said. "Rutter is coming unglued, he's unraveling, looks like he's starting to talk to himself."

"Oh God! What did I get myself into," Lance said as he stood on the pitcher's mound with the eyes of the sports world zeroed in on him. "I should have stayed on the farm where I belong."

"Oh, oh...It don't look good," Billy said.

"Your father and the Dodgers are going to beat the Yankees, Billy," Brent Heven said.

"That's right, Billy," Trent Heven said. "Your Dad is more than capable. You just watch, Lance and the Dodgers are going to win and it's not going to happen because of any angel magic."

"Have faith, Billy," Regina Heven said and then gave Trent a look that asked-- do we know what we are talking about?

Maura asked Torre if she could go talk to Lance. Torre said he thought it was a good idea and he would call Lance into the dugout. Maura said that wasn't necessary, she would go out to the mound and talk to him as was traditionally done. She grabbed her crutches and made what was a long walk for her to the pitcher's mound. The bases loaded, a twelve year old girl ventured out to the hill to try and calm down her farmer father! Meanwhile, Joe Torre had the presence of mind to step out of the dugout to check on Billy. He saw a six year old with a hot dog in one hand and a soda in the other laughing and enjoying himself with Trent, Brent and Regina.

"Are you ok, Billy? Torre asked.

"We got our eye on him," Regina said. "We will take care of him."

"Thank you for everything," Torre said. "You're heaven sent."

"What does he know?" Trent said to Regina.

"That's Lance Rutter's daughter walking toward the pitcher's mound," Joe Buck said. "Joe Torre hired her as Lance's personal pitching coach. I talked with her before the game. She's a beautiful twelve year old girl, smart as a whip, I'd say she is of genius caliber. She has Muscular Dystrophy but you can't tell her she can't physically do something. She will find a way."

When the crowd realized who she was they gave Maura moderate applause. Maura slowly made her way to the pitcher's mound one crutch step at a time.

"I got myself in a real pickle didn't I, Maura."

"Nothing you can't handle, Dad. Tell me, did you eat today?"

The question perplexed him. "What's that got to with anything?"

"Dad, you always told me you have to start with a good foundation and then follow through with your meals. Please tell me what you ate today."

"I gave the consigey guy a few avocados and he gave them to the cook and they made me avocado pancakes and tea for breakfast. It was delicious. Not as good as you make though, Maura."

"The consigey guy, who is that, Dad?'"

"The man in the lobby behind the desk who gets you what ever you want."

Now she knew what her father meant. "Oh, the concierge, that was a good idea, Dad."

"For lunch I had two big ABLT sandwiches, avocado, bacon, lettuce and tomato. I've got the avocado slices that you brought in the dugout if I get hungry."

"That's good, you've eaten well," Maura said. "Dad, you have everything in you to pitch well. You can control the game if you control yourself. I know you're nervous, you have never pitched before this many people before. You have to block all of them out. Just think about making someone special who isn't with us very happy."

"God?" Lance asked.

"Two people then, God and Mom," Maura said. "Pretend you're in the back yard throwing to Russell. All the Yankees look like him so it shouldn't be that hard."

Lance laughed. "That's funny, Maura."

"I don't know what Maura is saying to him but she's got him smiling and that can't be bad," Joe Buck said.

"Dad, you're bringing your pitching arm elbow above the level of your shoulders. You don't want to do that. Also, concentrate on pointing your glove directly at the target, this will keep your shoulders closed. That's all you have to do. These are the only things you should be thinking about. Do you think you can remember that, Dad?"

"I think so, Maura. It's only two things."

"Oh one more thing, Dad, word in the dugout has it Opple said you were a Mamma's boy."

"He's not smiling anymore," Joe Buck said.

"He certainly isn't," Tim McCarver agreed. "He's got his business face on now."

The bases were loaded, no outs and David Opple was coming to the plate. The New York press dubbed him the Big Opple. He was cocky, confident, capable and callous, a perfect fit for the high octane Yankees. A center fielder with an arm like a cannon and a mouth to match. He was leading the major leagues for most home runs, RBI's, throwing assists, and expletives. The Big Opple was a big man with a bigger ego.

Most of the Dodgers in the dug out were giving sunflower seeds an oral workout. Maura and Torre were nervously eating avocado slices.

"These are delicious, Maura."

"They're also very beneficial and good for you, Mr. Torre, you'll see."

The Big Opple stepped up to the plate. "OK, avocado man, let me see what you got. It don't look like much from what I saw so far. So let's have a go at it."

Mamma's boy Lance thought, *I'll show him.* Lance wound up, *keep pitching arm below shoulder level, keep glove aimed at target,* he said to himself.

Lance threw a curve ball that started low and right of the plate. Then, way right of the plate, about three feet from it, the ball rose, curved and caught the center of the plate. Opple never attempted to swing, seeing it start out so right of the plate.

"Strike one," the umpire said.

"That's the curve ball I alluded to earlier," Tim McCarver said.

That broke more than a killer wave off of Half Moon Bay," Joe Buck said.

"Lucky pitch," Opple said. "Let's see you do that again.

Lance then threw a pitch the exact opposite of the last pitch. It started three feet from the left of the plate, it was high, then it curved downward and crossed the strike zone in the center of the plate. Once again Opple made no attempt at swinging.

"Strike two," the umpire said.

Opple mumbled to himself.

"It seems like you lost your eloquence Opple," Russell Martin, the Dodgers catcher said.

"That's a trick ball," the Big Opple said. "I never seen nothing like that. He's using a trick ball."

"Let me see that ball, catcher," the umpire said. The umpire took the ball and studied it for a moment. "Looks like a normal baseball to me," he said, "don't look like Raytheon built it. We'll hold onto this." He tossed the ball to an MLB official and said, "Give this to the

Commissioner." He gave another ball to the catcher who threw it to Lance.

The Big Opple stepped back in the batter's box. He was wearing his swing for the fences face.

"I'm gonna airmail this ball, Rutter," Opple said, "to Los Angeles."

Lance threw a ball that headed straight down the middle of the plate. It curved away from Opple, and Martin, the catcher, had to move to his right to catch it. Opple swung.

"Strike three!" roared the umpire.

"You otta dar, Big Opple!" Billy screamed.

"Can I see that ball?" Joe Girardi asked as he came running out of the Yankees dugout.

"Sure," the umpire said.

Joe Girardi mumbled to himself as he examined the baseball.

"I've never seen a Yankees team that was so tongue tied," Russell Martin the catcher said.

Lance struck out the next two batters to end the inning.

"I don't know what his daughter said to him," Tim McCarver said, "but it should be studied."

"Whatever buttons she was pushing were the right buttons," Joe Buck concurred.

In what turned out to be a pitching duel between Lance Rutter and CC Sabathia the game was scoreless heading into the ninth inning. Sabathia had struck out nine, Rutter had struck out twelve. Joe Girardi sensed Sabathia was tiring and sent in the closing sensation Mariano Rivera to stop the Dodgers from scoring. Rivera struck out the first two players. Lance was batting next, and he had struck out twice already. Joe Torre was flashing signs. "Watch for the bunt," Joe Girardi yelled from the Yankees dugout. The infield moved in. Rivera threw a cutter fastball that lingered over the plate. Lance Rutter had been waiting all his life for this pitch. He swung and got most of it, the ball was hit straight out to center field toward the Big Opple who turned and started running back to the wall. Opple leaped, the ball just missed his glove. Lance Rutter had just hit his first home run in his professional career. A tirade of expletives flowed from Opple's mouth.

The rest of the Yankees were quiet, the stadium was quiet, and then, "That's my Dad that hit that home run over the Big Opple's head!" Billy screamed. Lance rounded the bases and was eagerly greeted by his Dodgers teammates. The Dodgers were leading one to nothing.

Rivera got the next batter to ground out.

The World Series was going into the bottom of the ninth inning with the Dodgers leading one to nothing. Lance Rutter looked liked he had gotten steadily stronger as the game progressed. Joe Torre decided to leave him in the game. Lance struck out the first two batters. One more out and the Dodgers would have upset the mighty Yankees. Lance threw a curve ball to Derek Jeter that came close to hitting his jersey but didn't and on a questionable call the umpire said he was hit. Jeter took first base. The winning run was coming to the plate. It was the Big Opple.

"OK, farm boy, I've seen enough," Opple said. "You put that avocado anywhere near the plate and I'm gonna make guacamole out of it and you can take your two brats home and play in the dirt. You don't belong here, Rutter. You should be in a carnival. You're a freak."

"I'll show you something freaky," Lance said and started to dig into the pitcher's mound with his spikes.

"Maura, can your father get this loudmouth out one more time?" Torre asked.

"Yes, Mr. Torre, he can. Can I go out and talk to my father?"

"Sure, Maura, go ahead."

"Thank you for believing in my dad, Mr. Torre, and for all you did for this family."

"My pleasure," Torre said as he handed Maura her crutches.

Maura looked at the crutches and handed them back to Torre. She got up unassisted and walked up the dugout steps.

"I'm ok, Mr. Torre!" Maura started walking without her crutches for the first time in many years of her short life. It had been about ten years since she could walk on her own. Lance saw her walk toward him, and he realized she was walking without crutches. He made a motion toward Maura.

"No," Maura said and held up her hand. "Stay there, I'm coming."

"Here comes Lance Rutter's daughter again," Joe Buck said. "She's walking without crutches. If I remember correctly the World Series program given to all those in attendance today states she hasn't been able to walk on her own since she was two years old. How inspiring is that?"

"You're correct, Joe," Tim McCarver said on the internationally televised program, "I have my copy right here."

The activity among the fans grew. Some showed those around them the article on Maura and pointed to the paragraph about not walking on her own since she was a baby.

"That is incredible," Joe Buck said. "What a marvelous feat to witness!"

"The fans have started to realize what has happened and they were now reacting," Tim McCarver said. "Listen to the applause!"

The applause grew thunderous. Everyone was standing, people tried to get a better look, some tried to get closer, many took pictures and recorded the event, a sea of cameras and recorders created a flash festival.

"Wow," Billy said, "I never seen my sister walk without crutches."

"Oh, Billy, I'm so happy for your family," Regina said as she gave Billy a big angel hug.

Maura approached her father. Lance Rutter dropped his glove on the mound got on his knees and embraced his daughter. Maura hugged her father as hard as she could. Tears streamed down Lance's face. "My baby is walking, My little girl can walk. How did this happen, Maura?"

"We were blessed," Maura said.

"Thank God. Thank God for miracles," Lance said, his voice choking up with emotion.

"It's fantastic, Dad, and we will celebrate this moment later. Dad, right now I want you to concentrate. I want you to do something. We have unfinished business here. We have a job to do." Maura put her hands on her father's face while he was still on his knees .

"What do you want me to do?" Lance asked.

"I wonder what this sweet, innocent, lovely little girl is telling her father now?" Joe Buck asked.

"Dust him!" Maura said.

"What?" Lance asked.

"Dust him! Knock him down. I want to see The Big Opple kissing dirt!"

"I could do that, but... You think it's ok, Maura?"

"Yes I do. Don't hit him... but come real close. Knock him down, then throw him a right hook, a left hook and finish him with the freight train."

"Oh, Maura, I don't know if ..."

"Look at me, Dad." Maura held her father's hands. "No room for negative thoughts. Yes you can. Yes you can. Yes you can."

"I can! I will!"

"She's got him convinced he can do something," Tim McCarver said.

"Right hook, left hook, freight train in that order, Dad."

"Right hook, left hook, freight train. Yes I can!"

"Make us proud, Dad."

"I will, Maura." Lance picked up his glove and stood up. Maura walked backed to the dugout.

"Look at the expression on Rutter's face," Joe Buck said.

"He looks like a man with a mission," Tim McCarver said. "His daughter's going to make one fine motivational speaker some day."

After getting up from the knockdown pitch Opple wiped the dust off his lips and offered an outburst of profanity that prompted the umpire to issue a warning. The next pitch Lance threw Opple a sweeping curve that hooked inward as it got close to the batter and crossed dead center of the plate. He threw another monster breaking ball that hooked at the last second and just caught the right corner of plate. Lance's last pitch of the World Series was a fastball right down the middle!

Peter Paul Licata

The Big Opple seem to forget how to swing the bat as he took all three pitches.

"Strike Three!" the umpire proclaimed a bit gleefully.

"He's throwing voodoo balls," Opple said. "He's a freak I'm telling you. He and his kids are aliens." Opple's pants came loose and dropped to the ground where they tightened around his ankles.

"I'm going to have to cite you for indecent exposure," the umpire said.

"The Los Angeles Dodgers have won the World Series!" said Tim McCarver. "They won it on the arm and bat of an avocado farmer from Fallbrook, California. That is some accomplishment for Los Angeles."

"I'm still trying to sort out what we have just witnessed," Joe Buck said. "This World Series win for the Dodgers is a major achievement, and yet it pales in comparison to Maura Rutter walking without crutches for the first time in years."

Billy and the young angel were embracing each other and yelling, "We're number one!"

"What part of this were you involved in, Trent?" Regina asked.

"Nothing. No part," Trent said.

"Are you sure, honey?" Regina asked.

"Just the pants at the end, dear, I couldn't resist."

"Nice touch," Regina said with an impish angel's smile.

"Congratulations, Billy," Trent said. "I wish we could stay longer but we must be going. There was a flood in China. They need our help."

"Bye, Billy," Regina said with a wave.

"I think we will see each other again," young Brent said. "Good-bye, my friend."

"Good-bye," Billy said.

The Stadium was quiet, the Dodgers were not. Billy climbed on the dugout roof and yelled, "My dad is a World Series Hero!" Lance Rutter looked for and found Billy. He ran over to the dugout and hoisted Billy onto his shoulders. Maura walked to her father and her brother. Lance lifted Maura in the air while balancing Billy with the other arm. The crowd applauded. They too were part of history. They knew they had witnessed something special, something magical. The Rutters acknowledged the applause and made their way for the locker room surrounded by adoring Dodgers players and coaches.

"Listen to that," Tim McCarver said.

"I hear it," Joe Buck said. "The home team fans are applauding for a performance like none they have ever seen. I think that says it all. ABC's Sally Derwell has managed to get to Joe Torre and she's got a question or two for the Dodgers' manager."

"Congratulations, Joe," the reporter said, making eye contact with Joe Torre and speaking into her microphone. "You've won some World

Series before. How would you characterize this one?"

"Special. Very Special. On so many levels."

"Does Lance Rutter practice voodoo?"

"Not to my knowledge, Sally," Torre said with a chuckle.

"How does Rutter make the ball do what it does, Joe?"

"I wish I could answer that. I can only say Lance is a very hard worker and when he is focused it's amazing what he can do."

"How does it feel to beat your former team, Joe?"

"It's sweet. It's large."

"Joe, I was trying to get a word with Lance and he quickly went to the locker room."

"He doesn't seek the limelight," Torre said. "He's not that kind of guy. He's a big family guy."

"That's some family, the cute little boy, and his daughter...she's something else," Sally said.

"She certainly is. She's the big winner," Joe Torre said..

"Thank you, Joe."

"My pleasure, Sally."

"Guys, there's some very happy people down here," the reporter said, "back to you, Joe."

"We have witnessed some extraordinary events," Joe Buck said. "We have seen greatness and goodness. I couldn't be more happy for the Los Angeles Dodgers and especially for the Rutter family. Thank you all for sharing this special moment with us. Good Night."

The Rutters were sitting on the front porch a few days after the World Series, still trying to comprehend and sort all they went through. What part did the angels have in it? How much did Lance actually contribute on his own? What made Maura's MD all but vanish? 'We were blessed," Lance said. "Your mother made friends with God and He blessed the Rutter family." Lance was happy with that reasoning.

A white Chrysler Sebring pulled into the driveway and stopped in front of the Rutter home. California Department of Children's Wellness was stenciled on the driver's side door. A pretty woman in a white pantsuit got out of the car. She walked to the bottom of the porch step, showed a badge and said, "Hello, my name is Joan Miller. I am the Executive

Director of the California Department of Children's Wellness. Are you Lance Rutter?"

"Yes I am, come have a seat, Joan Miller."

Joan took a seat on the porch. "This must be Maura and Billy."

"Yes, these are my children," Lance said.

"Hi," Billy said, "nice to meet you."

"Hello," Maura said softly.

"Congratulations! Mr. Rutter, you were spectacular in the World Series, and Maura, it was so uplifting to see you walking. You're both an inspiration. I wish you continued happiness. Mr. Rutter, there's another reason I came today. I wanted to deliver a letter in person."

Maura got nervous.

"The California Department of Children's Wellness has nominated Lance Rutter for Father of the Year. Here is a formal copy of the nomination." Joan handed Lance an official looking envelope with the California state seal affixed. "One more thing, Mr. Rutter. You sent me a box of avocados shortly after I broke the femur in my leg."

"I did?" Lance asked.

"I sent the avocados to you," Maura said.

"Oh, I see, Maura. Did you send them for your father? That was such a nice thing to do."

"I've been so busy lately I didn't realize you did that, Maura," Lance said. "Thank you."

"You're welcome, Dad."

"Let me tell you, Mr. Rutter, I was told my femur would take up to twelve weeks to heal. I was walking ten days after the accident and my doctors could not explain how I healed so quickly. I think your avocados had a big part in my healing process. Not only are they delicious, I started feeling better as soon as I started eating them."

"Your husband must have been quite surprised by the quick recovery," Maura said.

"My husband died four years ago," Joan said.

"We're so sorry," Lance said.

"Miss Miller, did you ever have avocado ice cream?" Maura asked.

"No, I never did."

"It's really good," Billy said. "Want some?"

"Just made a fresh batch," Lance said.

"I'd love some," Joan said.

"I'll get it," Maura said. "Billy, maybe Miss Miller would like to see the World Series scrapbook you made."

"Oh I'd love to see that, Maura. Mr. Rutter, you have a wonderful family."

"You can call me Lance."

"All right, Lance. It's beautiful in this area. I just love the country."

We'll show you the farm after some ice cream," Lance said.

Maura did her research and knew Joan Miller was single. Joan knew Maura wrote the letter for her Dad. Yet everybody seemed to like each other. Everything was all right.

Four Months Later...

The magic continued. The Rutter farm was harvesting award winning avocados which were selling at a premium and were sought all over the world. Lance Rutter was very charitable with the profits. Although Lance didn't seek the spotlight he acquiesced when he became the California Department of Children's Wellness Father of the Year. He was also selected Most Valuable Farmer by The Avocado Association of America. He and Joan Miller began dating and almost immediately became very fond of one another.

Maura remained healthy and ended up using her crutches to support tomato plants. She started working with the local, state and national MD organizations, and is currently helping others with MD through diet, exercise and sheer will.

There were many Rutter Avocado accomplishments and claims. A few of those:

Many reported better vision and hearing. Bones healed quicker. Minds got sharper.

Three year old Manuel Ortiz completed Saturday's *New York Times* Crossword Puzzle's Greek Edition.

Joe Torre now has a full head of hair.

Fallbrook, California secured a reputation as Avocado Capital of The World.

Ninety-two year old Emma Parkins said her dog now rolls over on command. This is quite a feat since Emma never had a dog.

Peter Paul Licata

The Big Opple entered a treatment center for people who swear too much. He wasn't (expletive deleted) happy about going.

Billy Rutter, aspiring magician, could now pull an elephant out of his ear.

Some magic can be explained.

Some magic can't be explained.

And perhaps some magic shouldn't be explained.

Let's just call it Avocado Magic.

The End.

About the Author

Peter Paul Licata lives in Scranton, Pennsylvania. He earned a Bachelor's Degree from the University of Scranton in Business Administration.

Avocado Magic is his second book. *GolfHead and the Grass Menagerie*, his first book, is also available at AuthorHouse.

Breinigsville, PA USA
04 August 2010
242987BV00001B/7/P